Why Is Your House Bigger than Mine?

By Latanya Lasha Riley

Mrs Lockleu,
Thanks for
supporting me!
I hope you
enjoy the
reading!
Latanya L Riley

PublishAmerica
Baltimore

ISBN: 1-4241-5533-9
PUBLISHED BY PUBLISHAMERICA, LLLP
www.publishamerica.com
Baltimore

Printed in the United States of America

Dedication

This book is dedicated to the generations of African American and minority students who have lived in the ghetto and not known the historical reasons, "Why?" It is devoted to: those students who never understood why "mama" and "daddy" both had full time jobs yet still lived within the perilous gates of what American society has deemed as an unsafe environment that breeds at-risk children, poor schools, single-parent homes, little or no social capital, drugs, violence, and hopelessness; to all the textbook writers who never published this data...the truth...for teachers to teach and kids to learn; and last, but not least, this book is dedicated to those persons who never knew, realized, or acknowledged how privileged you truly are. Learn, live, and then learn some more.

To my nieces and nephews, Charles, Jr., Chastity, Carlos, Kennedy, Karrington, and Kortlyn, who will have the perseverance and thirst for knowledge to learn about issues that will not be discussed in textbooks...go out, compare, question, research, and learn as much as you can. Questioning is the fuel that keeps you wanting to learn more, and more...and more.

Acknowledgements

First I would like to thank my heavenly Father for all the great things He has done for me. Every word and every thought of this book is attributed to Him. I give all my love and gratitude to the following persons: the Riley family for being my foundation; Nathaniel Riley Jr. for motivating me to pursue my dreams and not give up; Dr. Alfredo Artilles for being such a thought-provoking professor and opening up the dialogue in the classroom to discuss issues that many professors shy away from; Ayana Brown for changing the way I thought and articulated about social issues of inequity that were relevant to me; my class members from SPED 3820 at Peabody College of Vanderbilt University; Mr. Davenport, for the great poem that you shared with me for this book; all of my girls, Kim, Maurika, Kesha, Arkia, Kendra, Cassandra, and Sharica, thanks for believing in me. FCC baby!; my teachers and professors, thanks for building my academic foundation, being great role models, and sharing the knowledge that is still with me to date; and to Dr. Judith Presley, no matter how much I forget to keep in regular contact, I will always admire you…your style, your grace, your intelligence.

Thanks…

Author's Note:

Why is Your House Bigger than Mine? is a fictional narrative in which Sydnee Jenkins, a young precocious twelve-year-old from one of Detroit's most destitute neighborhoods, learns just why she lives in the ghetto, while all of her classmates live in the more affluent suburbs. When an argument sparks between her and a classmate, Sydnee, along with her intellectually endowed classmates, begins to understand the true meaning of the "privileged" and the "underprivileged," and the difference between what is "equitable" and "equal." This quarrel opens up the doors of learning that can not be found in a textbook, and it gives her teacher the autonomy to either teach about the issues or disregard the history that explains to us about White flight, blockbusting, redlining, and racial segregation that even exists to date.

Introduction:
The Old Times

I can remember my childhood like yesterday. Everything I did is still a vivid snapshot in my memory. I have to say that my childhood friends and I were very innovative. We were modern day inventors, or at least we thought so. We didn't have a lot of things to do in my neighborhood, so being the kids that we were; we would make up all types of inventive games to play. Anything that brought us joy became routine for us. I remember the hot summer days when my friends and I would play the notorious hand games, *Down, Down Baby and Twill, Lill, Lee.* Every little Black girl in the country knew them, played them, and sung them. These were games that had been passed down almost like Negro spirituals to all the little Black girls in America.

If we were lucky, our parents would let us walk to the local community center to watch the neighborhood majorettes practice. Marching to the beats of the bass drums, putting on that glamorous uniform trimmed in the gaudy designs, and wearing those dainty white boots, was every little girl's dream in my neighborhood. But unfortunately, due to limited funds for so many of us, it was just that-a dream. Many of our parents couldn't afford to pay for the uniforms or the boots, but that didn't stop my friends and me. We would race home from the community center, run back to my apartment, grab the extension cord and radio that played five minutes after it was unplugged, and rush back outside. We'd plug up my granny's old raggedy radio, connect the bent wire hanger, which was now a makeshift antenna, in hopes that the sounds would come out a little clearer.

"Come on Sydnee! Twist the hanger on there good, shoot. Hurry, up!"

While I was getting the radio ready, my friends would be standing in formation. And finally, "It's on, y'all! Y'all, ready!" That music would come blasting out of the radio like the TSU Aristocrat of Bands at the beginning of one of their halftime shows, and there we would go, dancing like our ancestors probably did back in Africa, only we had a little more rhythm and a lot more hip hop dances.

By the time our parents would call us in the house, we would've made up our very own majorette dance routine, incorporating the *Pop Shake*, the *Roger Rabbit*, the *MC Hammer*, the *Kid-N-Play*, and a few other dances that we had seen the majorettes doing down at the center. We weren't official majorettes, but in our eyes we were just as good. If only we had the money and a sponsor, we would have been da bomb!

As kids we lived to play outside together, to walk to the candy lady and buy freeze-cups, pickles, two-cent cookies, and to play on the playground. Going to the candy lady, was like going to the grocery store for us. On the days that we went to the candy lady, we would all run in the house and beg our parents for change. If they didn't have it, we would search for it under the pillows of the couches, the loveseat, in dresser drawers, in old worn clothes, anywhere until we had enough money to make a purchase.

Unfortunately, we couldn't enjoy the outdoors as much as we wanted. There was too much crime, too many gangs, and too many people in my neighborhood that couldn't be trusted, especially around kids. But I must say that my friends and I did have tons of fun. I still love those girls, Kesha and Tameka. We were best friends to the end, but we ended up going our separate ways around middle school.

My mom sent me to a magnet school on the "White" side of Eight Mile, and they attended our neighborhood school on the "Black" side. We really didn't have time to spend together anymore because before long, my mom had me in all types of extracurricular activities...*Girls-2-Girls* on Mondays and Wednesdays, the After School Program on Tuesdays and Thursdays, and on Fridays, I was at the library checking out new books. The only time I really saw Tameka and Kesha was when I walked home from the bus stop. They would be outside enjoying their preteen years, talking to the boys that my mom had forbidden me to converse with. Me, I would be in the house doing homework, skill and drills, or helping my granny with house chores.

When I look back on things now, I must say that I'm glad my mom was the way she was with me...strict, yet loving because my two best friends now have three kids each, and we are only twenty-one years old. I'm sure that's overwhelming for them. Whenever I come home from college break, my mom and I just sit around and talk about how things have not changed, and how so many of the kids I grew up with, were held back by perilous temptations that came along with living in what's known as the "ghetto" to the bourgeoisie and the "hood" to inhabitants.

To my friends, I was a hero, superwoman, "Sherra." I had made it out...out of the ghetto! I was in college pursuing my dreams of becoming a doctor.

"Sydnee, girl, we are so proud of you. You're doing your thang! If only we had a strict mama like Ms. Jenkins, we'd be just like you. You know she wasn't playing that. There was no hanging out or chillin'' for you, and, boys...yeah right! That was out. Yo mama made sure you stayed in them books. Girl, you lived in them books!" We all laughed.

"I know y'all. She was strict."

"You should be glad, though. At least you're not like us, still living in these raggedy-old projects. Your mama was determined to get y'all out of here, and she did. Just be happy, girl. You are truly blessed."

"I know. I should. I just wish you all could be with me. We would be a bad team together."

"Oh, we know. We were unstoppable back in the day."

"Like my mom said, 'Tameka and Kesha should have gone to school with you. They would've had fewer distractions with them being in a better environment.'"

"Yeah, Sydnee, you know she's right."

"You went to that 'White' school up in the suburbs. You had opportunities at your school, girl. The teachers cared. Girl, you actually had books that weren't used by yo' mama when she was in school. Yo' teachers believed in you."

"Come on, now. So, did yours! What's that teacher's name who used to shop down at that African bookstore? She seemed like a good teacher."

"Oh, don't get me wrong. She was a good teacher, but she alone was not enough to inspire seven hundred plus kids with personal issues, family issues, reading issues, and money issues. Need, I go on?"

"I catch your drift, Kesha."

"We're just saying Sydnee, your teachers had high expectations. They prepared you for college. Most of our teachers were garbage. They prepared us to be good workers, not good leaders. And besides, after you went to Cadillac Junior High School, shoot you blew up. After you and that White guy, finished informing Detroit about the 'burbs and the projects, y'all were meant to go to somebody's college. Shoot, they already had scholarships in y'all's names."

"Come on, now. That's not true."

"Come on, Sydnee. Yes, it is. After you went to Cadillac, you were officially on the college track. You were prepared for those hard classes, unlike us. Whatcha' call those classes…A-something."

"A-P."

"Yeah, that's it, A-P. While you were off on your college track, we were in vo-tech classes learning how to cook and clean, lay carpet and bricks, do somebody's nappy head, or fix someone's car that we would never be able to afford to drive. We were learning dumb stuck…stuck that would make us cater to rich folks."

"Having a trade isn't dumb stuff! I wish I had learned one. A trade is a guaranteed job. That's something that no one can take away from you. Besides, with a trade, you can start your own business."

"O-kay, well, not dumb stuck. How about 'this job will keep you with a low paycheck type of stuff.'"

"You are crazy!"

"Come on, Sydnee. You know we were learning stuck that limited us in some ways. You know?"

"Yeah, I guess. But, I hate I didn't get a chance to go to Richards with y'all."

"Honey, you didn't miss a thing. Be glad you didn't go to Richards."

"Yes, I did. I missed the socializing aspects of middle and high school. The kids at my school were cool, but they were not like the kids from around here. Y'all, know that. It was two different worlds. It was like night and day, ebony and ivory. It was totally opposite. We'll have to finish talking about this later. I have to go girls. I have to go pick up my mom from work."

"Good luck, Sydnee. Don't forget about us when you blow up. Okay?"

"Y'all know I'd never do that. Come on, y'all know we're F-C-C for life." F.C.C. stood for Friends Connected through Christ. We called ourselves that because who else had the power to keep three friends safe from all the dangerous elements in our neighborhood. Nobody, but Him!

"We love you, girl!"

"I love y'all, too."

As I walked back to the car, I became very teary-eyed. I didn't understand why I made it out of Magnolia Park, and they still lived here. I mean these two girls were my home girls, my road dogs, my sisters, my posse. We were like the *Three Musketeers*. I began to think about everything that we did together as kids and about how, now, we all lived different lives.

Living in the hood was and still is a cycle for many people, and the only way they get out, is if they fight their way out. If you lived in the ghetto, you had to fight statistics, fight society, fight the powerful, fight temptations, fight capitalism, fight oppression, fight for opportunities, and fight for your own dreams. And they wonder why we are so aggressive. Maybe my mom was right when she sent me to Cadillac Magnet. At the time, I wasn't happy about it at all. I couldn't understand the fact that all schools were not the same, or that there are the "better" and "best" schools within a city. You'd think that public education would mean equal education, but that's all a big myth, a political dream. It may be equal, but definitely not equitable.

For example, it's equal for all kids in public schools to have books to read. However, it's inequitable when the rich schools have the latest textbooks, but the poorer, usually inner city schools, have textbooks that were assigned to their cousins who're ten years older than them. It's equal that all kids have schools to attend. It's inequitable, when some kids' schools look like miniature college campuses with the most modern technology; and poorer schools look like miniature prisons with windows you can barely see through, or schools that their ancestors attended because you still have air conditioning units sticking out of the window and the closest thing to technology is the intercom the principal is barely heard through. Many kids all across the country in the poorest neighborhoods know that, 'if you lived in the ghetto, your school looked like a factory if you were lucky and a prison if you were not so fortunate.' Your books would probably be considered antique if they were appraised. The computers were probably older than you, if you even had them in the first place. And most of the teachers were not really teachers. The district couldn't find anyone else who was certified, so they ended up settling for less qualified teachers.

However, if you lived in the suburbs, schools were great, and it they were clean. You didn't have to share books with three other people. The computers didn't have spider webs and rust growing on them, and the teachers were as they would say today "highly qualified." The only thing that was equal was the amount of grades all students completed-Kindergarten through twelfth grades.

I can remember it like yesterday, but I must say that Cadillac Magnet taught me a lot about life, history, destiny, beating the odds, and ambition. I can still recall the discussion I had with my mom about not wanting to attend school there, my startling journey to school through the most stunning side of Detroit I had ever seen, and the first day that has changed the way I think about the rich, the poor, the ghetto, the suburbs, the privileged, and the not so privileged.

Chapter 1:
Good School, Bad School

The summer had finally ended, and tomorrow was going to be my first day as a 7th grader. I was getting older. I was becoming a young teenager with more odds to beat, more doors to knock down, and more people to prove wrong. This year I was really going to have to buckle down on the books and study. I promised myself that I was going to end the year with perfect grades. I wanted all A's. There was no room for B's in my life. Besides, my mom had transferred me to a new school, Cadillac Magnet Junior High School, named after the city of Detroit's founder, Antoine de la Mothe Cadillac. I still didn't understand why she transferred me to this school. I would not be with my girls, Tameka and Kesha, anymore. This was going to be the first time we'd be separated. Personally, I didn't see anything wrong with my old school. It was named after a famous person too, Ms. Fannie Richards. She was Detroit's first African American school teacher, kindergarten teacher, and founder of the Phyllis Wheatley Home for Detroit's elderly and poor Black citizens. And may I add that Mrs. Richards along with John Bagley, a wealthy tobacco manufacturer, were the first to integrate Detroit Public Schools. From the looks of it, I would think that my old school was the better school, but my mom thought otherwise.

She insisted that the teachers were unqualified, the books were old, half of my peers were at-risk, and to top it off, the school was one low-test score away from being taken over by the state. Yet still, I didn't see what the big deal was. To me, there wasn't such a thing, as bad schools or bad teachers, but there was a such thing as bad students and parents. Personally, I felt that if all the students from a "bad" school were placed in a "good" school, then that school would become "bad" too. And if all the "good" students were placed in the "bad" school then what was once the "bad" school would now become the "good" school. I know that sounds weird, but that was only what I thought. I saw the teachers struggle, day in and day out with some of my peers. I heard them attempt to phone some of the parents who were unresponsive, defensive. And, I witnessed them trying to bring up-to-date information from textbooks that they had used in school when they were students and making ends meet with little to no school supplies for us to use. I saw their relentless efforts going down the drain, and I watched how day after day, the gist of our instruction time went to discipline problems. I mean, "Who wouldn't have the perfect school without kids with discipline problems, with supportive parents, stable home environments, recent textbooks, an ample amount of supplies for each child to have his or her own, and other issues that most teachers would never understand?" But that was only a thought that lingered within my mind.

As I lay on the floor with my head resting on my purple beanbag, the electric fan housed in the living room's window, blew cool air onto my face. During the moments when the fan rotated away from me, I watched my mom iron my new school clothes. This was the first year that I actually had brand new school clothes, but I only received these because we were required to wear uniforms at my new school, which was another minus. Who wanted to wear uniforms? This school took away from my individuality, and I hated it already. My mom effortlessly ironed my white blouse until there were no more wrinkles. "Sydnee, pour me some more water in a cup for the iron. I need to finish ironing these pleats in your skirt."

"Are you sure mama? You know what happens when you feel up Grandmama's iron with water."

"Girl, come on. I don't have all day. This iron has not been leaking that brown stuff lately."

14

"Oookay."

It's a good thing my skirt isn't white because I would be out of luck. Mama knows that once she puts that water in the iron, it's going to start leaking. And the residue is going to leave little brown water spots everywhere. Shoot, you'd think that iron was barbecuing the water or something! How in the world does water go into the iron clear and come out dirty brown. Talk about metamorphosis! Anyways…whatever.

As she meticulously ironed each pleat, the stem from my grandma's iron filled the air. It reminded me of the smoke the police cars made when they were chasing the neighborhood criminals. Before long, every curl in my mom's hair began to flop. The more she ironed, the straighter her curls became, and the thicker her edges grew. Her forehead began to bead with moisture from the steam. And she just kept wiping, and kept on ironing. The more I watched her, the more I began to laugh.

"You'd better stop laughing because starting next week, you'll be ironing your own clothes. So take notes now, and laugh later."

"Please don't make me, Mama. I promise not to laugh."

"It's too late for that, my dear."

Far in the distance, I could hear my grandmama's old clock ticking. When I looked up, the time was nearing 8:30pm. "Five, four, three, two…one."

"Sydnee, it's time for you to get ready for bed." I knew my bedtime signal was coming, and it came promptly at 8:30-on time. So, I grabbed a washcloth out of the laundry basket, skipped down the hall, and leaped over the floor furnace right into the bathroom. I flicked on the light, turned on the hot water, and wet my towel. As I waited for the water to get hot, I begin to sing my favorite song, *The Battle is the Lord's* that we sing at church on Sundays.

"There's no paaaain Je-sus can't feeeeel. No-ooo hurt, He can-not heal. All things work accor-ding to His per-fect will. No-ooo mat-ter what you're go-ing through, re-mem-ber God is u-sing you. For the bat-tle is not yours. It's the Lord's"

I sung this same verse every night as I prepared to wash my face because I knew that the water would finally be hot by the time I finished singing the last word in the verse. As I picked up the washcloth to squeeze out the water, "Bam," just like I thought! The water was hot just the way I wanted. "Dang, I'm good!" So, I began to bring the towel up towards my face for my nightly cleansing. Then, "AAAAAAAHHHHHH!"

"Girl, what is wrong with you in there!"

"Get the broom, Mama! There was a spider on my towel, and it almost got on my face."

"What?"

"It was on the inside of the washcloth, and it almost got on my face when I got ready to wash it!"

"Where did it go?"

"I slung it down there on the tub somewhere!"

Before I knew it, my mom had turned into the exterminator, and saved our life from the horrifying arachnoid. If she keeps that up, she could probably get a job as the Orkin wo-Man.

"Mama, what was he doing in the basket with our clean washcloths, anyways?"

"He must've come from those dirty washers and dryers downstairs. I wrote a letter to the Authority last week about those spiders, and so did Ms. Jeffries. They ain't never going to clean up down there. I've got to get us out...of...here, and fast, before this old decrepit place kills us first."

After that incident, I rushed and washed my face. I could still feel my heart racing and hands shaking. I threw the towel on top of the shower head, popped off the light, and ran into my bedroom. I pulled down the White vinyl shade to my window, pulled back my covers, popped off the lights, and jumped in the bed pulling the covers up over my head.

"Make sure you say your prayers, Sydnee."

"Oh shoot, I forgot to pray again! Dear Lord, please keep away all evil as my family and I sleep. Please let my mom have a good day at work and school tomorrow, and watch over my granny. And Lord, please let me like my new school. Don't let any of the kids tease me, and let my teachers love me. One more thing Lord, please keep the spiders out of the projects and let us get out of here soon. Amen."

Chapter 2:
Getting Ready for School

"Syd-nee! Sydnee, get up girl!" Get up! Wash your face, brush your teeth, and come eat your oatmeal."

I could hear my mom yelling from the kitchen as I rubbed out an old night and rubbed in a new day into my big brown eyes. It was barely 5:15, and I had already been given a chain of commands.

I slipped out of the bed and walked back down the hall to the bathroom. My mom had already prepared my washcloth nice and hot for me, just the way I liked it. For fear of encountering another spider so close to my face, I double-checked the towel for any evidence of rodents, bugs, or spiders. "Thank, God!" There were none there. Besides, I didn't want to start my first day of the new school year with a bug in my face, some luck that would be.

"Girl, you need to prime yourself for your first day at your new and improved school."

"Mama, I still don't understand why I have to go to a school all the way on the other side of town."

"Sydnee, didn't I tell you it was going to be a better school, and most importantly it was going to give you a much better education than these old city schools?"

"But mama, you can't measure education."

"Oh yes, you can."

"How do you measure education? Just because I go to a school with better test scores, doesn't necessarily mean that I will learn more."

"Yes, it does. Now, all of your teacher's time will not be centered on discipline and getting students up to grade level because these students already have manners and they are at or above grade level. At this school there are less discipline problems, therefore there will be more learning going on. Annnnnd, there will be enough books to go around. So, you won't have to share. Okay?"

"Yeah, mama. I guess."

"Yeah, mama?"

"Yes mam, mama."

"Don't be giving me any lip, young lady. You are going to go to school, and you are going to have a good day, okay! Now go in the bathroom, and grab your hair bucket, so I can comb your hair. Comprende!"

"Comprende, mama."

This was a battle that I had definitely loss. There was no use in me playing the devil's advocate with this one. Well, I guess I should look on the bright side. At least, I was about to get that good ole-fashioned, kitchen hairdo. That was the best. I was about to be transformed.

As I positioned my little wooden stool between my mother's legs, she placed the straighten comb on our old white *General Electric* stove. But don't let it fool you. Although this stove was ancient, it carried out a lot of jobs for us. It cooked our food, made our hot water, heated us in the wintertime, and like now, it heated up the comb to convert my hair from being wooly and thick to straight and silky. As the fire heated up the comb, my mom parted my hair in sections, and greased my scalp with the *Blue Magic* hair grease. It took her all of about 15 minutes to press my hair. I was amazed at how much body I had. It was startling how my hair went from being immovable to moving like the mane of a horse. It went from short to long with the command of heat. Next, she parted my hair into two sections, and gave me two long ponytails, both held with my new red hairballs. My ponytails were so long, that they looked like bunny ears.

"Shirley Temples or Rudy Huxtables?"

"Shirley Temples, please, Mama. I am going to junior high. It's enough that I'm wearing these pigtails to junior high. Now, I wouldn't dare wear plats!"

'Shirley Temples' were the long spiral ringed curls, and 'Rudy Huxtables' were braids. When she finally finished, she wiped the extra grease from around my hairline, and told me to go look in the mirror to see if I liked it. I rushed to put up the stool, ran down the hall, jumped up on the vanity, and stared at myself in the mirror. Once again, I was amazed. How in the world did she manage to get my edges so straight.

"I love it, mama."

"Good. Now…, will you have a good day at school?"

"Yes. I sure will!"

There was something about getting your hair pressed that made all the little Black girls across the world feel special, feel different, feel like a superstar. It was now 6:00 am, and my mom and I were out the door and on our journey to the bus stop. I was catching bus route 416 to River Rouge just north of Eight Mile Road, and she was catching bus route 379 to downtown Detroit, south of Eight Mile.

Chapter 3:
On My Way to School

As I boarded the bus, I still didn't understand why I had to travel so far just to go to school, especially when my neighborhood school was walking distance from my house. But my mom said this was going to be a better school. So I was holding her to her word. As the bus voyaged through the city streets, I watched as Detroit's landscape abruptly transformed right before my eyes. I was amazed. I had never seen this side of the city. Suddenly the city didn't look like the city as I knew it, anymore. Everything that was distinctive of the city had vanished. The projects, the train tracks, the liquor stores, the raggedy cars, the homeless, the graffiti, and the beauty supplies had all disappeared.

"Where in the world am I going? I couldn't possibly have boarded the right bus. Oh man, I am on the wrong bus." As these thought ran through my mind, I became very anxious and somewhat afraid. It was my first day of school and I was going to be late because I boarded the wrong bus. I had to do something and quick! So I got up from the torn green seat, and marched up to the front to tell the bus driver about my stressful predicament.

"Excuse me. Excuse me, Mam! I think I have boarded the wrong bus." The driver began to laugh. As she laughed in my face, I looked at her like she was crazy. What in the world was so funny? She is trippin.'

"Baby, what bus are you supposed to be on, child."

"Well, I was supposed to get on bus route 416 to the River Rouge area."

"Well, you are on the right bus, dear. I know it can be confusing sometimes. When you travel south of Eight Mile, it's hard to believe that you are still within the Detroit area. Don't feel bad, child. People north of Eight Mile do it all the time because we are used to living on the 'ghetto' side of Detroit where everything looks old and ramshackled."

As I swaggered back to my seat, I could hear the bus driver chuckling feverishly. I guess this was a scenario she had witnessed and clarified for her fellow patrons more than once. As I took my seat, once again, I began to stare out the blurry window in disbelief. It was so beautiful. There were gorgeous flowers, lively emerald grasses, big beautiful shade trees, clean streets, luxury cars, huge houses, and smiling faces.

"Oh, my! Look at that big yard they have!"

It was nicely manicured and full of Bermuda grass. The shrubs were nicely shaped, and the mulch was well distributed around the flowerbeds. I would love to dwell here. I bet the kids play outside all day and night, unlike the kids in my neighborhood. We always go in when the streetlights come on. I wished I lived here. That's okay because when I graduate from medical school my family and I will live better than this…in due time.

The bus stopped on River Rouge Parkway to pick up more passengers. This time a tall, slender, and very frail man came to sit next to me.

"Is this seat taken?"

"No."

I wished it was taken. I pulled over my bright red backpack that my granny bought me, and he slithered down onto the seat.

"I see you're enjoying the scenery."

"Yep. It's really nice. Looks a lot better than my neighborhood."

"Mine too."

"What do you mean? Don't you live out here?"

"No. I wish. What made you think that?"

"Well, you did board the bus on River Rouge Parkway didn't you?"

"Yes, but I transferred to that point from another bus route. I work out here. Did you see all the nicely manicured lawns?"

"Yes, I did. They were beautiful!"

"Well, I did that. That's my job. I call myself a Landscape Manicurist." We both laughed. Some name I thought.

"So do you make a lot of money?"

"Living wage."

"What's living wage?"

"It means I make more than minimum wage, but less than I need to prevent myself from struggling. Besides, the nicer I am, the more gifts, tips, and bonuses I get. Can't beat that!"

"I guess. Look, that's a good-looking car."

"Bingo!" said the man.

"Bingo?"

"Come on now, I know you've played Bingo before. That's the game that po'folks like us play whenever we come to this side of town."

"But, why?"

"Because to have these things you must be a lucky person. These are things that a lot of us will never have, you know. It's only a dream. At least if we play Bingo, we can say it's ours in our mind."

"Well, I don't have to play Bingo. When I graduate from Harvard's School of Medicine in 2019, I will have things that are much better than this."

"That's very good. I love to see motivated little sistahs. Keep it up baby girl. Make those dreams your reality. I wish I had."

When the next eye-catching car passed, I was amazed. "Bingo!" Before I knew it, I had made the car mine. We both laughed in amazement.

"Next stop, Cadillac Magnet Junior High School!" The bus driver shouted loud enough for me to hear her. I guess she wanted to make sure I didn't get confused this time.

"See ya' later, Mister…!"

"Mr…, Mr. Boyd. It was good conversating with you. That's a new word I learned yesterday while cutting this rich lady's lawn." We both laughed. "Have a good day at school. Knock 'em out for the rest of us, Black Folks, baby girl."

"I will. See you later!" I should have told him the word's conversing not conversating, but he said it with too much confidence. I would have hated to bust his bubble.

I hopped down off the steps of the bus, and onto the decorated sidewalk that led up to the school's front door. Before now, the only decoration I had seen on a sidewalk was graffiti. But not here, the decorations were intended to be there. Each sidewalk had a different inspirational quote for us to read as we strolled up to the school, and a beautiful school, might I add. It didn't look like the factory and prison-like schools in the city.

This school resembled a mini college. There were different buildings, and each building had its own name. There was the School of Arts and Social Sciences, the School of Math and Science, the School of Music, the School of Language Arts, and the School of Primary and Foreign Languages. The last building was reserved for the cafeteria and P.E. classes. But, "What sense does that make?", I thought. There can't be this many kids here. Just as that thought came over me, I remembered what my mother said, "Baby, the student teacher ratio is eight to one."

This explained why the school was so immense and spacious. As I walked past each block in the sidewalk, I slowed down and read each quote. *If opportunity does not knock, build a door* by Milton Berle. *You must do things you think you cannot do,* Eleanor Roosevelt. *Invest in yourself, in your education. There's nothing better,* Sylvia Porter. *Formal education will make you a living. Self- education will make you a fortune,* Jim Rohn. And last but not least, *We were born to succeed, not to fail,* by Henry David Thoreau.

"Duuh," no wonder this is the best school in Detroit. Who could possibly become discouraged after reading such encouraging words everyday before and after school? I was so excited. I could not wait to get home to tell my mama about everything.

Chapter 4:
Within the Walls of Learning

As I entered through the big red doors of Cadillac Magnet Junior High School, I was flabbergasted. The school looked so friendly and warm. I loved the colors. The walls were decorated with beautiful drawings ands more motivational quotes. There had to be hundreds of quotes all throughout the school. "I love this school already." All of the teachers were standing outside their doors greeting the students.

I didn't know where I was going. I was just walking slowly through the halls admiring the scenery. I should've expected this after seeing the beautiful scenery on my bus ride here. As I followed the signs towards the 7th grade hall, I marveled at all the neatly dressed kids. Although most of them had on name brand clothes stitched with horse and little alligators, I still was the neatest. The pleats in my skirt were perfectly ironed, my shirt was crisp, and my new *Pony* tennis shoes were glistening. And to top it off, I was equipped with my newly pressed hair and Shirley Temple curls. Just looking at me, you would have thought that I was from the River Rouge area, but I wasn't. As I neared the end of the hallway, I heard someone speaking to me.

"You must be, Sydnee?"

"Yes, mam. How did you know?"

"Well, I just have that special teacher's touch. I know all about my kids before they even enter my classroom." She ended her remark with a very friendly smile and a pat on my back. "Go on in. You are on the first row, first seat, with the pink hat."

I went on in the class. Unlike my old school, to my surprise, the class was equipped with enough computers for each student to work individually. As I looked around I noticed that I was the only African American in the class. "Why, isn't this the melting pot?" I couldn't believe it. There had to be more gifted Blacks in Detroit than just me. I mean dang there are more Blacks in special education classes than this. So, what are they trying to say about my people? I guess Mr. Boyd was right. As he stated, I was going to have to knock 'em out for the rest of the Black folks.

Promptly at 7:30, the tardy bell rang and Mrs., ...Mrs. Umm...I didn't even catch her name. What a flop! Well, the teacher closed the door and stood in front of the class, her audience for the next 180 days. Oh yeah, well I guess I wasn't the only African American. The teacher was African American as well. Good, because I was beginning to get worried.

"Good morning, class. I am Ms. Dream and I will be your teacher for the next 280 days."

"What in the world is she talking about?"

Ms. Dream was the most petite teacher I had ever had. She was very short, only about 5'1", and she was in shape. It looked like she was a regular patron to Powerhouse Gym. And her hair, I loved it! It was cut in a layered bob, just like the lady from the Black Hair Magazine. It was a dark auburn with light auburn highlights, and her hair was full of body. It moved even when she blinked her eyes. She wore a long sleeve blue buttoned-down shirt with a white collar and silver cuff links. And to liven it up, she had on this Black knee length skirt, off-Black stockings, and some Black heels that resembled a man's loafer. She looked life a teacher from the early 40s, but I must say she did look hip and professional at the same time.

"For those of you new to the school, or who didn't know, we are going to be a year- round school this year."

"Ahhh, man. Great."

"So I will be seeing a lot of you all. And I am truly looking forward to working with each and every one of you. Before we began, I have to take the role. When I call your name, raise your hand, stand, tell us your full name, something about you, and where you live. I know most of you all live in this beautiful neighborhood, so tell us what subdivision or mini community. And for those of you new to the school, tell us about your last school. Let's get started. Okay, first is Taylor Appleton."

What, most of the kids are from the neighborhood? For the first time, I was embarrassed to say where I was from. I had never been around other kids who weren't from my neighborhood. I had never been around rich kids. The closest I came was watching the Olsen twins on *Full House*. Everyone's rich. Oh, God! Help me! I have to tell all these rich kids were I'm from. I'm going to confirm the stereotype that all Blacks live in the ghetto. Please, God, let her mistakenly skip me. I need you right now, God. Besides, they may laugh when they realize I'm from the projects.

Everyone had gone over his or her autobiographies. I sat in bewilderment as they described their lavish lifestyles, their parents' knock-out jobs, their flawless families, their safe neighborhoods, and their awesome summer vacations. The last name called was Jackson, and that was the seventh student. And I was number eight, Jenkins.

"Next, class is Sydnee Jenkins."

My blood raced through my veins and directly towards my heart. I became extremely nervous, and suddenly very hot. But for some strange reason, there wasn't a drop of sweat anywhere on me.

"Sydnee, come on sweetie. The class is waiting for you."

She was right. Everyone's eyes were on me. It was like they knew I was going to deliver some bad news. Yet still, I sat there motionless and quiet. Then all of a sudden, I got up, ran straight from my seat, and straight out the door. I'm sure the class was quite baffled. They probably asked themselves, why I ran out on such an easy assignment-another stereotype of my race- lazy. But I didn't care. I kept running right through the door. Once in the hall, I slid down along the wall onto the newly waxed floor. I covered my face with my little caramel hands and felt the tears of embarrassment race down my little brown face.

Ms. Dream came out the room, and closed the door behind her. "Sydnee, what's wrong dear?" I still just sat there motionless. "Sydnee, I need for you to talk to me. Tell me what's going on."

As I began to raise my tear-coated face, I noticed the quote on the opposite side of the hall. *Never give up. A true winner overcomes adversity.* Just when I needed it, I thought.

"What is wrong Sydnee? I can't help you unless you tell me."

"I don't want to introduce myself. I refuse to become the laughing stock of the school."

"What are you talking about? Has someone been teasing you?"

"No! But they will, as soon as they find out where I'm from."

"What do you mean?"

"Ms. Dream, I don't live such an extravagant lifestyle. My mom and I live with my grandmother in the Magnolia Park Projects near the corner of 30th and Michigan Avenue. And occasionally my aunt and her three kids come to live with us when her husband kicks her out or beats her up. Our house isn't anything that a person would want to share or brag about. My house isn't this huge five-bedroom mansion with two kitchens, four bathrooms, a playroom, and a triple car garage. Plus we don't even have a pool. There is supposed to be one, but all the drunkards and people who don't care about Magnolia Parks have filled the pool with trash and other debris. My neighborhood is not safe like River Rouge. There are drive-bys, drug deals, and kidnappings everyday. And the police don't do anything about it. And as far as my old school, that is off limits. It's just as worse as my neighborhood, and it will never compare to this school. Besides my mom said my old school was one low-test score away from being taken over by the state."

"Well, Sydnee, people come from different places and situations. It doesn't matter where you come from. What matters is where you are going. Everyone will never have the same lavish lifestyles or the same blessings. And believe me, I know."

"But at least you don't live in the projects, Ms. Dream."

"No, I don't Sydnee."

"See."

"But, I used to live there. When I was a little girl, my five siblings and I with my parents lived in a two bedroom in Memorial Gardens."

"Really?"

"Really. When I was a child, I was embarrassed to tell people where I was from too. I would lie and say that I was from Warren. But it wasn't until I matured, that I realized the real reason why I was there with many other African Americans."

"What's the real reason?"

"Sydnee, I'll have to tell you about that a little later, but now, I want you to go wash your face and come back to finish your assignment. Go ahead, the rest of the class and I will be waiting."

"Can you give me a hint, Ms. Dream?"

"Just know and understand that God didn't make the ghetto for us, the government did."

"The government?" I was baffled. I didn't understand. What was she talking about?

"Come on, sweetie. We'll discuss this a little later, okay?"

"Okay." Ms, Dream was down! She said God's name in school! What! That's what I'm talking about. She doesn't have to worry about me reporting her. I'm down too!

Chapter 5:
The Confession

"Okay class, quite down. Let's listen to Miss Sydnee."

Okay, here I go. "Sorry…no I apologize for my leave of absence. Anyways, hello, my name is Sydnee Denise Jenkins, and that's Sydnee with two e's. This is my first year, here, at Cadillac Magnet Junior High School. Last year, I attended Fannie Richards Middle School, and now I am just starting to realize how much I miss my friends, Tameka and Kesha. This is the first year that we will not be attending the same school. My mom transferred me here for the gifted program and because she thought my old school was low performing and not challenging me enough. I am the only child, and I live with my mama and grandmother in the Magnolia Park Projects on the south side of Detroit."

Once I made it known where I lived, I noticed that a lot of my classmates began to whisper and giggle. I was not going to let them belittle me. I had to regain my strength and be strong like my granny had taught me. So being the strong Black young lady that I am, I asked, "What is so comical about what I said?"

Everyone got quite. You could hear a pen drop. I wasn't sure if they were quiet because I had used a big word, or if they were quiet because I scared them.

"Okay class, let's be respectful." Ms. Dream tried to spare my feelings, but I was fine now. Besides, I had been praying for strength. I wasn't going to let anyone break me. Then, all of a sudden, this chubby kid proclaimed, "She lives in the ghetto!"

Before I could even stick up for myself, this tall skinny girl beside me stood up on my behalf. "James, you don't know where she's from. And even if she is from the inner city, it's none of your business to judge her. How dare you!"

Sounds good to me, I thought. "What's your name?"

"Hi, Sydnee. I'm Reagan. Pleased to meet you."

"And I'm Sydnee. It's very nice to meet you, as well."

Reagan was very frank. With the help of her extremely elaborate vocabulary, she spoke her mind, and wasn't scared to stand up to anyone. Her poise was breathtaking. When she talked, everyone listened. I bet her parents were lawyers or something. She was tall and thin with long blonde hair. She wore it pulled back with a navy ribbon. I could see her years from now standing, up for women's rights, human rights, everyone's rights. The girl was impressive. She probably had the potential to do anything she wanted. Then, here goes that chubby kid, James, with his thoughtless remarks again.

"Well, Reagan, you did a good job trying to stand up for civil rights, but my dad said that anyone who lives in the projects is poor and lazy, and our hard earned tax dollars are being spent to support their dismal lifestyles. Now, I'm positive my Dad wouldn't lie to me! He never lies to me."

"Well, James, first your tax dollars are not being spent because you don't even have a freaking job. And secondly, it looks like your father is as ignorant as you are!"

Way to go. This girl is good. She should be a lawyer. Tameka and Kesha would love her. She could be the fourth member of the Three Musketeers. I can tell Reagan and I were going to be the best of friends.

"Okay class let's stop these little shenanigans! James you are out of order. Not all people who live in the ghetto or inner city, for that matter, are poor and lazy. How would you feel if I said, all the people in River Rouge are racists. That wouldn't be true, would it?

"No, mam."

"Exactly. What you did and what your father told you are called stereotyping or stereotypes." Ms. Dream went to the board and wrote down the word, s-t-e-r-e-o-t-y-p-i-n-g. Anytime a teacher wrote a word on the board, I knew to write it down. If it was worth her walking to the board, then I knew it had to be important.

"And stereotypes are nothing more than fictitious or untrue generalizations about a person or group of people. Anytime you hear the words, *all* or *most*, then the red light should go off in your mind that a stereotype is probably about to follow. Let's just pause for a moment. We have to address this issue, right now! I cannot allow these sweeping statements to go on in my classroom and not address them."

The class stopped and listened.

"When I was your age, I had this very same problem, and it's not right. My siblings and I were teased because we were from the projects. But my fifth grade teacher did this great activity that I will never forget that explained to us why some things were destined to happen. So pick a partner. James, I want you to work with Sydnee."

The class was quiet. Everyone could tell that Ms. Dream was greatly saddened by what had been said. Even James looked a little remorseful, and I didn't feel alone anymore. There was actually someone in this school who could identify with my environment and me. Yet still, I was furious. My blood was boiling and that James was lucky that Ms. Dream had stopped the class because I was going to give him a piece of my mind. But on the other hand, I felt sorry for him because his dad had fed him so many absurd lies. How dare he say that people from the projects are lazy? My mom works two full time jobs and goes to school part time. She is far from lazy. As Ms. Dream passed out the construction paper, crayons, and markers, I wondered how in the world was art was going to solve this problem.

"Okay class, I need you all to take about thirty minutes to draw a picture of your neighborhood, and on the back write a brief description describing it. Include the types of people you see, the atmosphere, and the surrounding businesses you may find in your area. When you finish, swap papers with your partner. I want you to look carefully at their drawing and examine it. Note anything that catches your attention."

I could not figure out why Ms. Dream had us doing this senseless assignment. This was not going to explain to the class why I lived in Magnolia Park, and why they lived in their little rich neighborhoods. Besides, this would be the perfect assignment for them to further judge my neighborhood and me for that matter. Now, they would get to see it first hand through my drawing because I was going to draw Magnolia Park exactly the way it was.

Once I started sketching my neighborhood, I really began to realize how awful it really was. Nothing I drew depicted vibrancy or happiness. All the people looked depressed, the streets were covered with oil from old beaten-up cars, and the buildings were all run-down. It was hard to believe that many of the people who lived here, actually worked full-time jobs, and this is where working two full time jobs had gotten my mother and I.

The more I drew, the sadder I became. The more I wrote, the more depressed I felt. I couldn't understand why I lived there, and they lived here? As I glanced around the room, I noticed that most of my classmates were happy as they doodled away at the drawings of their perfect neighborhoods.

"Class, when you all are finished, you all may walk around and observe others' drawings. And while you are walking around, look for the similarities and differences in each others' drawings."

Since I was finished, I figured I would give it a shot. I wanted to see just how many of my classmates' neighborhoods came close to mine. I walked slowly by each person's desk. "Humm, close. Taylor lives in an apartment, and so does Maxwell." Finding that out, made me feel a little better.

"Sydnee, do you see anyone whose home is similar to yours?"

"I noticed that Taylor and Maxwell both lived in apartments, too."

"Good, see. It's not so bad after all."

"Well, actually Sydnee this is a condo. Maxwell and I live in the same complex," Taylor stated.

"Sorry, maybe I was wrong, Ms. Dream."

"Not really. Apartments and condos are very similar. They both are contiguously built, meaning that each apartment is not separate from the other."

"Well, what's the difference?"

"I know, Ms. Dream!" said Taylor.

"Okay Taylor, well tell Sydnee the difference."

"Well, actually when you live in a condo, which is short for condominium, the tenant or person who lives there does not always pay rent. In some cases, the person pays a mortgage, like on a house. In an apartment the tenant pays rent to the owner of the apartment complex. So the tenant actually loses money because he or she cannot acquire…I forgot what it's called. I heard my dad talking about it with one of his friends.

"Equity, Taylor," Ms. Dream said.

"Yeah, that's it…equity. And they can never own an apartment."

I was confused. "What is equity?"

"Well Sydnee, my dad said it's the money that you get from your house. For example, when you move in a house, it may be worth seventy-five thousand dollars, but after you live there for some time, say ten years, it may be now worth one hundred thousand dollars. So you have just gained twenty-five thousand extra dollars."

"Oh, I see. So my mom is paying rent only to make the owner rich."

"Yep. Well, actually Sydnee, in your case, the receiver is the government because the government owns the projects," said Taylor.

This girl was a natural whiz kid, and she was extremely knowledgeable in real estate. Maybe her dad was a realtor or something. She was petite and very pretty. Her eyes were the color of the sky on a sunny day, and her hair was long, blonde, and wavy. Her skin looked very soft, not too oily. She had a special glow about herself. She kind of looked like that actor Brittney Spears who plays on the Mickey Mouse Club. I'd buy a house from her any day.

"Hey Taylor, thanks. You and I are going to do business one day. Maybe you can be my personal realtor, when I get ready to buy a house? You know, help me with making the best decisions." We both laughed.

"No problem, Sydnee. I'm sure the extra money will help out. Maybe I can give it to my kids for their allowance." We both laughed.

I finished walking around observing everyone's drawing. Those who didn't live in apartments, or condos, dwelled in big pretty houses.

"Man, White people are really rich. Look at the flowers and big yards. My, what nice cars and joyful faces they have." I nearly wanted to play Bingo just looking at their pictures.

"Okay class, let's bring it to a close. Exchange papers with your partners. Each person will present their partner's illustration to the class."

Chapter 6:
Oh, NO!

James and I were the next to last duo to present. When it was time for James to introduce my drawing, I covered my hands in my face. I knew I was the only one with an unpleasant neighborhood.

"Hello, I'm James, and I will be sharing Sydnee's drawing with you all."

"Okay James, before you start, let's go over a few guidelines. Make sure you elaborate about anything that stands out in the picture to you. And explain why it stands out. Okay, go ahead."

"Well, from the looks of it, Sydnee lives in a high-rise apartment building. I noticed over here and down there, that there are a few shattered windows. I also see a lot of trash on the ground. For some reason, it looks like the playground has been taken over by adults. But, why? That's rather peculiar. Well, I also noticed that she has the sun covered by dark clouds. This stands out the most to me. It looks as though the sun is trying to wrestle its way from behind the clouds. Hmmm…I…I don't know. To be honest, I don't understand this. Could Sydnee explain it for me and the rest of the class, Ms. Dream?"

"Okay James, but first, let's see what the rest of the class thinks, said Ms. Dream."

Taylor raised her hand. "Maybe because it rained a lot there."

"Well, that could be a possibility, Taylor. Anyone else?" No one else raised their hands. I knew no one would understand. James came close but he still had no idea. They weren't on my level. We were from two different backgrounds. They couldn't possibly understand my struggle. They're all from the rich suburbs. They would never understand.

"Okay Sydnee, you're on," said Ms. Dream. I stood up and cleared my throat.

"O-kay. Over here, is my apartment building. The two buildings beside mine, are buildings B and C. I live in building A. My building is exceptionally old and worn. There are broken windows everywhere, and that's because the passerbyers have thrown bottles through them. And of course, some have been shattered by gunfire. Over here, is what used to be the playground. As you can see, there are no kids out playing. If you look closely, you can see that the kids are in their apartments looking out the windows. We're afraid to come out and play because the playground has been taken over by drug pushers, gang members, and other people who are too dangerous for us to be around. The gang bangers call it their turf. But, we do go outside occasionally to play, only if a parent is out to watch us. This man down here by the door is Big Wayne. He always tried to clean up the neighborhood, but unfortunately a gang member murked...I mean killed him a weeks ago after word got out that he had been talking to the cops. The sun is not shining, purposely. I made it this way because there are never happy days in my neighborhood. Everyday seems gloomier than the one before. Everything seems dark and hopeless. So that's why the sun is not out. All the paper you see on the ground is trash. Everyone litters. They think the neighborhood is nothing but trash, so why not? All the way back here in the background is the expressway. To me, this is just not any old expressway. To me, this expressway is an escape route out of the inner city, away from all the problems and all the bad stuff that lives here. And last but not least, if you look closely in this window, you can see my family and me looking towards the sky. Well actually, we're looking up towards God. My granny always tells us that God will make everything okay, and not to give up hope or faith. That's it. Any questions?"

No one raised their hands. "Okay, that's it. The End."

When I finished, the class was mind-boggled, shocked, sad, and very sympathetic, but really, no one new what to say. I wanted to do like Spike Lee did at the end of *Do the Right Thing,* WAAAAKKKKEEEE-UPPPPPPPPPP!!!!

"Is that really what your neighborhood looks like Sydnee?"

"Pretty much, James."

"So you never get a chance to go out and socialize with your friends?"

"Nope. Never."

"See class, this is exactly why you should never tease one another because you never know another person's struggle," said Ms. Dream.

"I'm sorry, Sydnee, for being immature and saying that very stupid comment to you."

"No problem, James. Now you know, and I expect that your thoughts will change from here. Right? Maybe you can even inform your dad, huh?"

"Yeah, maybe."

Although James and I started off on the wrong foot, he was a good guy. I knew he couldn't have been as mean as his words were. He just didn't know, and not knowing can cost a person a lot in life.

Chapter 7:
Revamping

Everyone still seemed reluctant. After witnessing my drawing and listening to my very in-depth description, no one wanted to talk about their drawings or their neighborhoods for that matter. I guess they didn't want to feel like braggarts. But I didn't mind. I was no longer ashamed. I wanted to see the differences in the way we lived. That, to me, was learning, and learning was what I was here for.

Yet still, no one volunteered. So, Ms. Dream decided to break the ice.

"Okay, since no one wants to go, I'll pick someone." Everyone sighed hoping she wouldn't pick them. "I see no one wants to present, so I'll pick someone's to present. And the lucky person is going to be..."

Ms. Dream paced around the room, up and down every aisle, pecking her pen on her jaw.

"...Ashley."

Just liked I expected, Ashley's home was the exact opposite of mine. Unlike me, Ashley lived in a spacious brick mansion, and in her description, Ms. Dream said, "And Ashley says, it resembles Brandon and Brenda's house from the show 9-0-2-1-0."

"9-0-2-1-0, my God, that is a huge house!" Ashley's house certainly was large. She had her own bedroom, bathroom, and a walk-in closet. Shoot you could barely walk in your kitchen let alone a closet! She had a pet dog named Daisy, and both her mom and dad had their BMW and

Lexus parked inside the double garage.

"You all must be rich, girl. I'd love to live there. Your parents must be zillionaires."

"Well, actually, Sydnee, my dad's an orthodontist and my mom is a stay at home mom."

"Stay-at-home mom. So you're telling me that you all got all of this from one little job. Okay, well not a little job, but from one paycheck. Shoot, my mom works two jobs, and we still live in the projects. Something ain't right. Something isn't adding up."

"Well, maybe your mom's income doesn't add up to what my daddy makes, said Ashley."

"But my granny works, too. She works down at the cleaners, ironing clothes."

"Okay girls, let's stay on task. We'll have to do a lesson on economics another day."

"We sure will. Shoot, I'm trying to live like them, Ms. Dream!" Ashley probably thought I was crazy for adoring over her and her family like that. But that was amazing. They were living the life. That's the life, us, people from the ghetto dream about.

"Ms. Dream began to talk again, "We have to stop here today, but for homework, I want you all to go to the library and find as much as you can on the specific type of neighborhood that you reside in, or you may surf the Internet when you get home, but make sure your parents have your Internet filtered from any explicit material that may pop up, if you know what I mean? Okay, anyways if you live in the suburbs, find information on the history of the suburbs. If you live in an apartment, find information on the history of apartments. If you live in a condo, like Ms. Taylor or Maxwell, then look up the history of condos."

"What about the projects, Ms. Dream?"

"I was getting their Sydnee. And if you live in the projects look up the history of the projects. Better yet Sydnee, look up history on the Public Housing Authority because that will give you more information. Any questions class?"

"Sydnee, has a question."

"Thanks, Taylor."

"I really have a comment."

"Okay, comment, questions, they're all the same, said James."

"I think this is a great assignment, and I think it is heading in a great direction, but I don't think I will be able to make it to the library."

"What about the Internet, Sydnee?"

"Come on James, do you really think I, have the Internet? We don't even have a typewriter, let alone a computer."

"Oh, yeah, I guess you're right. Sorry."

"Okay, back to me. Why can't you complete the assignment, Sydnee?"

"Ms. Dream, because my mom doesn't like me going out after 4 o'clock. That's when the sun begins to set, and when the sun sets, the hoodlums come out. And besides, Mrs. Smith, the librarian closes at 4:30 because she likes to be in her car with the doors locked before it gets dark and the hoodlums forget who she is."

"Okay. Will someone remind me when 2 o'clock gets here? Since everyone doesn't have access to the library, we will stop whatever we're doing, and start our research then. But you all have to promise me that you will collect enough information because when you all get home, I want you all to summarize your findings. And make certain, that you summarize it thoroughly. I want paragraph form and complete sentences. This will be journal one of your journals. When we come to class tomorrow, each person will discuss their findings, and we will bring this lesson to an end. Besides, this will be a great way for me to get a feel for each of your public speaking and writing styles. And plus, I have to research as well. Is that a deal?" In unison the class agreed, "It's a deal."

"Thanks Sydnee, for getting us out of some of our homework."

"No problem, James. Whose to say I won't need you later on?" We both giggled. I raised my hand up to give him high-five, but he just left me hanging. "Jaaammmmess, I was trying to give you high-five."

"Oh, sorry. I didn't see you."

"Hi-five."

"HI-FIVE."

Chapter 8:
Waiting for an Answer

I couldn't concentrate on my math assignment for thinking about my newly assigned research project. I couldn't wait to see what I would find. Plus, I was eager to share the end product with my mom and granny. "Come on, two o'clock," I said to myself as I watched the clock ticking, ticking away." It was only 1:57, and waiting for the three more minutes was going to take an eternity.

Finally. "Ms. Dream, it's 2 o'clllooooock!"

"Okay class, stop whatever you are working on. Taylor, take up the math work, and put it in the red tray on my desk."

"Row one, line up. Row two and last, row three."

I couldn't wait to get in line. The walk from the class to the library was liberating. Now, I know what Harriet Tubman must have felt like each time she traveled the Underground Railroad. I couldn't wait. I would finally find out what this project was really meant for. The library was over in the Language Arts building. We had to walk outside, pass the math and science building and travel up from the cafeteria. Boy, this is a long walk. I hope it's worth it. Finally, we were at the library.

"Okay, I want you all to remain on your best behavior. Go in, and complete your assignment. Don't waste anytime because time will go by fast. Is that understood?" As she said that, she had that 'I'm not playing with y'all look,' going on. That was the look my mama gave whenever she meant business. From the way we said, "Yes, Mssss. Dreeeam," it was also a look they had seen from their mom's as well. I guess that look wasn't a Black mama's look. I giggled to my self.

"Good," said Ms. Dream.

We went on in the library and scattered into our separate ways the same way the roaches did whenever my granny opened the kitchen cabinet, and they knew she was going to try to kill them. We went to work.

After about an hour and a half of researching, Ms. Dream took us back to the classroom to wind down for the day.

"I hope you all used your time wisely. And I know…I just know that everyone will have a lot to share tomorrow, right?"

"Right!"

As I rode the bus back on my long escapade home, I enjoyed the same pattern of beautiful scenery that I had enjoyed earlier that morning, at least until I reached the city lines. Only this time, the pattern was reversed. First, the beautiful houses with the big yards, then the welcoming public park, the shopping centers, the mall, the apartments and condos, then the fields. Now we cross over the notorious Eight Mile Road. From here are the interstates, the railroad tracks, the abandoned buildings covered with Vanilla Ice posters, advertising his new album's release date, the Save-A-Lot, the liquor stores, the drunkards, and now back to Magnolia Park where the kids were rushing home to avoid danger and the gang bangers from recruiting them.

I walked slowly off the bus, dragging my backpack down each step of the bus. I turned, waved to the smiling bus driver, and then walked up the rutted pavement to my apartment building. Believe it or not, the sign still read, "Welcome to Magnolia Park, where Dreams are fulfilled, 1939." Yeah, right. There are no dreams being fulfilled around here, more like nightmares. The door to the building was still broken, hanging from its rusty hinges. "Thank God! It's broken!" I did not want to put my hands on that dirty handle. It was too dirty for a pig to touch. As I walked in, I noticed the elevator was still broken too.

"Great!" I had to walk up five flights of rat-infested steps. Plus the stench was out of control. "Pewee! They need to clean up this place!" As I neared the fourth floor, I had already counted five people asleep, better yet drunk, in the stairwell. And by the time I reached the 5th floor, I was about to pass out from exhaustion and that horrible, horrible smell.

Once in the house, I went to eat my dinner that my Granny had prepared for my mom and me before she went off to work. She cooked everyday before she left because she knew my mama would be tired after working two jobs and going to class. Plus, she figured I would be starving after finishing a long day at school

It wasn't unusual for me to be at home alone. My mama worked and so did my granny. They had to make ends meat, bread, money. Besides I only had to stay at home until 5:00 when my mom and granny arrived here.

"I guess I'd better finish up my homework. Hmmm, let's see what this research says about the history of this crappy old building. As Ms. Dream puts it, let's see what it says about the Public Housing Authority, or P-H-A. That name's too fancy for this piece of crap."

As I began to read about the Public Housing Authorities' history, I became exceedingly puzzled. How could something that was intended to be for the good end up so bad? What happened to the government's help? Did they forget about us…the promised tax dollars? The more I read, the angrier I became. Hmmm…so there are different types of projects, huh? As I became more engulfed in the shocking rejoinders, I heard someone twisting the doorknob. Then I saw the doorknob turn. It wasn't time for them to be home yet. It was only thirty minutes pass four. It was too early. "Who in the world…?"

Chapter 9:
The Reasons

Thank God, I heard a key go in the lock. "Hey baby! How was my baby's first day at her new school? So do you like it?"

"No, mama. It was a terrible first day."

"Whatcha mean, baby?"

"Mama, why is everyone in the class house bigger than ours and why didn't you tell me that I was going to be the only little Black girl, who happens to be from the projects? Everyone else is loaded and lives in these massive houses that folks from around here can only dream of owning. And Ashley, her and her family, live in a mansion, Mom. To top it off, it looks like the house that Brandon and Brenda lives in on 9-0-2-1-0. And guess what else, her mom doesn't even work. Can you believe that? Her mom does-not- have a job. Nada. Nowhere. Nothing. So, I told them, that you have two jobs and grandma works, and we still live in the projects."

"Wait, a minute, wait-a-minute! Who is Ashley, Brenda, and Brandon? And what in the world is 9-0-2-1-0? And why were you all discussing each others' houses?"

"Ashley is a girl in my class, and Brenda and Brandon are the actress and actor who play on the sitcom, 9-0-2-1-0. And we ended up talking about houses because it was a part of the icebreaker Ms. Dream planned for us to get to know one another."

"Okay…okay. Well baby, first of all, you must realize that some people are more privileged than others. Some people have privileges that you and I will never have. That's why I keep telling you to do well in school, so that you can go to college, and get those same things one day."

"But still mama, why do we live here in these crappy projects?"

"Watch your mouth, Sydnee!"

"Why do we live here in these worthless projects, and they live there…in heaven? You have two jobs and granny works. That's three jobs, and Ashley's family lives off one job's check. How is that? I don't understand. It's not adding up."

"Well, baby, we don't have a choice right now!" I'm only getting paid minimum wage from the job at the hospital and after taxes, paying the rent, buying groceries, and helping your granny pay for her prescriptions, I just don't have a lot to save or buy a house with. And the other job, doesn't pay me. You know that. I'm only working at the GED place so I can go to school for free. Once I graduate from State, then maybe I'll be able to get a much better job, making more money, so I can get us out of here. I know it's taking a long time, but joy cometh in the morning baby! Joy cometh in the morning, and don't you forget that!"

"Good, I hope so. I hope it all works out. Well anyways, let me share some of my research with you."

"Okay, baby. Hit me, with what you've got."

"Well, did you know that this building's structure is considered a high-rise design and that it was first built to save the government from paying for a lot of land."

"What do you mean Sydnee?"

"Well, back then the government figured it takes less land to build up than it does to build out. You get it?

"Uh huh, baby."

"I also found out some other stuff too. It's kind of interesting but confusing at the same time. In one of the books it stated that projects built from the high-rise design, like ours, have more crime than the ones with less floors.

"Translate, please mam."

"Mama! Okay, tall projects have more crime than short projects." I hated when my mama did that. I felt like she was confirming some stereotype or something.

"Okay, young lady, don't be getting sassy. But, I can believe that. Look at the crime here and then look at the crime in Forrest Gardens. We outnumber them four to one. So, what are the other types of projects?"

"Well, in the notes I took at school, it states that there are garden projects like Forrest Gardens, low—rise, walk-up projects kind of like townhouses, and then there are home projects. Those look like a lot of little houses connected together...kind of like the ones that Kesha's granny used to live in. Then my notes also say that in the mid-70s, Congress stopped building high rises projects, the really tall ones, because they were fed up with all the crime.

"That's interesting baby. Too bad Congress didn't change that before they built this here dungeon, huh?"

"Yeah right, mama." We both laughed.

"So, what else does it say baby?"

"Let's see. On this page I copied from this book, it states that projects, which is also called the public housing authority, first was built for those people who worked in the city because many of the people lived far away in country or rural areas.

"What! Sydnee, you mean to tell me that they built the projects for people who had jobs. Huh! Isn't that something? Now, these projects are for us, people who don't have jobs or who barely make any money from the jobs that we do have. The government,...I tell you, is something else. For people who had jobs? Now, that's funny."

"But listen to this. It says that back in 1937, the government decided to give housing to the submerged middle-class."

"Sydnee, will you stop using these here big words. Say it so I can understand it!"

My mama hated when I used big words with her. She thought I was trying to make her feel bad, but really I wasn't. But, at the same time she wanted me to use big words around other people. Talk about wishy-washy.

"Mama, submerged means that something is like …swamped or flooded. You know how when the sewer lines get backed up downstairs in the laundry room. Then, all of a sudden everything is covered in the water like our clothes in the clothesbasket. You can say that our clothes were submerged with nasty sewer water. They were swamped. But in this case, we're talking about being submerged with people. Submerged means almost the same thing. But here, submerged means…like…over-represented. Like,…ummm…our neighborhood is submerged with drugs and crime."

The whole time my mama was looking at me like I was crazy. "Sydnee, I get the point."

"Mama, I was just making sure. Anyways, they wanted to help give places to live to families who worked but could not afford to live in fit houses. But then it gets confusing. It states that, "This was not for the poor who could not afford to pay any rent.""

"So, in a nut shell, Sydnee, the government wanted to let people who had jobs but not enough money live in the projects. What about people like Mrs. Lula downstairs on the 12th floor who cannot afford to pay any rent?"

Mrs. Lula was a sweet old lady who lived on the 12th floor. My granny said she moved here after her husband was killed from an injury he suffered at work. Mrs. Lula tried to sue her husband's job, but she lost because the lawyers said her husband died from a stroke. So, since she was disabled and had no job or money, she had to move here because she could live for free.

"Well, Mama, eventually, the government began to build or construct projects for those who could not pay rent. Read what it says right here."

She grabbed my photocopies and began to read. She stopped mid-sentence. " Initially, the projects were……really…beautiful. What? Come on now! I would have loved to seen that…the day the projects didn't look like a slum."

We both laughed again. "Yeah, that was hard to believe."

"Let me see that paper again. I want to read this." She took the paper back again and started to read. She couldn't stop.

"Listen, Sydnee. It says they interviewed a lady in Memphis who used to be over the housing authority down there. She said that four decades ago, in the 60's, her family moved from the North to some Memphis housing project. "

"And...?"

"And, she said that she was jealous of the kids who lived in the projects next to hers. She said that the projects next to hers called Lemoyne Gardens were the best projects in the city. They were had new playground, heat, hot water, anddddddd basketball courts."

"Dang, Mama! For real!"

"For real, baby! According to your granny, our projects used to be like that too. But over time, the government just stopped cleaning up around here, and this is what it turned into, a landfill full of crime, drugs, hopelessness, and filth. The projects sure have changed!"

"Yeah it's gone through metamorphosis." We both chuckled." Mama remembered that word because she helped me read about it once for homework.

"I just wonder, how did this place end up like this?

"I just told you how Sydnee. One day the government said, 'You know what, we can save all this money. Let them clean up their own neighborhood.' You know what Sydnee? I bet projects all over the country are like this old, run over, run down, cleaned out, and what's your word baby, ...di-lap-i-da-ted."

"Awww mama, stop. That's not my word."

"Well, it comes from your big list of vocabulary."

"For real though, did we get like this? Let me scan through this. I'm sure an answer is in here somewhere."

"Keep looking. I'm going to run to the back and get out of these clothes. Mama gots to get in something comfy, baby."

While my mom was in the back changing clothes, I looked through the papers as fast as I could. Here! "Mommmmmm! Mama! I found it."

"Here I come, girl. You scared me!" I could hear my mom rushing to get on her house clothes. She loved it when I dropped some knowledge on her. She wanted me to learn so I could teach her.

"Drop it on me, baby!"

48

"It's kind of hard to sum it up because it's so much."

"Just read it Sydnee!"

"Okay, okay. Calm down, Mama." My mom gave me that look. I'd better get to reading. I thought. *"After the war, the real estate industry forced Congress to reserve the housing only for the very poor. This later became what is known, now, as the Housing Act of 1949. In the 1940's and 50's, minorities made up thirty-nine percent of the people living in the projects, but in the 1970's minorities made up sixty percent. H*old on mama, let me look up 'minorities' in the dictionary.

I ran to the closet to get the Webster dictionary from the shelf. I thumbed through the pages..."M-a, ...m-e...m-i-n...here it is! Minority...*part of a population that differs from other groups in some characteristics and is often given unfair treatment, usually a small group of people within a large group.* So Mama, a lot of people would probably think that most of minorities are poor."

"Now, baby, I told you earlier, that some people are privileged and some are not. Minorities in this case, were not privileged. I can remember when I was a little girl just like you. My grandma and papa, who you never had a chance to meet, would sit and tell my parents and I about all the struggles they faced as a young married couple. Papa said he had just come home from the war, after four long years in Germany. He said that his fellow comrades and him couldn't wait to get back on American soil because they knew, greater things were awaiting them. As he flew back on the airplane, Grandma was headed to Virginia to meet him. She wanted to be the first person he laid his eyes on when he stepped off plane. Once they were reunited, they had big dreams. They were going to move away from the city. They wanted out of that little room they lived in."

"Room?"

"Yeah, baby. He and grandma lived in Buffalo, New York in a one bedroom apartment that they rented for three dollars a month from a White man who owned a shoe repair shop downstairs from them. But anyways, he and grandma had hopes of moving. With so many soldiers returning home from the war, they needed somewhere to live with their families. So the government began to build houses. Papa said they built thousands of houses in what they called neighborhoods, and what later became known as the suburbs, the 'burbs to us. Well, anyways, Papa was so happy because the government had built these houses for the soldiers to live in at a discounted price. I think Papa said the houses cost only seventy-five hundred dollars, but back then that was a lot of money. Today that's nothing if you can afford it."

"So, did granddad have the money to get a house for him and grandma?"

"Well, yes and no. The government knew that the soldiers couldn't afford to pay seventy-five hundred dollars so they passed what was called the New Deal or New Dollar Housing Act, or something. I think it was New Deal. But, anyhow, through this act the government with help fro banks wanted to give aid to help the soldiers pay for these houses. The banks said they would pay eight percent of the costs for the next thirty years. All granddad would have to pay was twenty percent which would end up being about a hundred and fifty dollars a year."

"That's all! I could've paid that."

"Exactly, so you see, Papa could have afforded it, especially after the income from his pension and plus Grandma worked as a seamstress. But to his surprise, these loans were only for the White soldiers and their families. So Papa and Grandma, along with all the other Black families were out of luck. They had to keep living in apartments or any other place they could find."

"That wasn't fair!."

"I know baby, and Papa knew this too. But there was noting he could do. So while the White families were enjoying their homes in their new little suburbs and getting rich, the Blacks were in the city getting poorer."

"Getting rich? How so?"

"Because when you buy a house, Sydnee, you gain, what they call equity."

"Oh, yeah, we talked about that in class, too. So in the end, Papa and Grandma were losing money because they couldn't acquire any equity if they lived in an apartment."

"Exactly, baby!" Plus, Papa had to buy things like refrigerators to keep the food from going bad, but the White families in the suburbs got theirs free from some company who made most of the appliances back then."

"So, I see, Whites could really do noting but save their money and get rich, while the Blacks had to pay rent, get no equity, and buy things that other people were getting for the hookup?"

"Basically. Now, do you see why some people are privileged and others aren't?"

"Yes, but I never knew things like that happened."

"Baby, that's something that you will never learn in school. That's what they don't want us to know about. They just want us to think we are supposed to be poor and them rich. To them, that is destiny. So even today, many Blacks around here think that the ghetto is where we are supposed to be. I mean we've been here for so long, it's kind of hard to think we belong anywhere else. But don't get me wrong, all Whites are not like that. Just like all Blacks aren't poor. Shoot, it just seems that way because when you go in any 'ghetto' in the country, who do you see? Us."

"But we don't deserve to be here, Mama."

"I know baby that's just the way it is. This is not the land of opportunities. We should be the land of the privileged."

"But, mom, at least we have more opportunities than some other countries. I guess we can be thankful for that."

"Yeah, baby we should. And you know what, this all makes a lot of sense when you think about it. Blacks came in this country as slaves. We were looked at as property. We weren't allowed to learn how to read or write because they knew that we would become a threat to them. We were powerful and smart without being taught. We were smart enough to learn anyways, and that was a great achievement for us. They knew, that given the chance, we would become even more powerful. Just look at how we tried to fight them off. I mean you've read the books. You read about how, some Blacks were clever enough to find the Underground Railroad and travel to the North for freedom. We know that, and so did they. That's why they recruited, us, Black folks to go to their wars and fight this country's battle. And sad to say, Blacks had to call it 'their' country too, but they knew when they returned home from war, that they would still be another outsider, another what you call those people who are not born here but move here?"

"Immigrants."

"Yeah, immigrant. You'd think that after helping to fight in the war that this country ended up winning, the least the government could do is provide equal housing for the same job well done. But, no! They did just the opposite. The Whites got the houses, and the Blacks didn't. The Whites got the handouts, and the Blacks got the hand-me-downs. The Whites got the equity and we got the rent. The Whites got the bigger houses and we eventually got the Public Housing Authority, which at first, wasn't even intended, for us. Like you said baby, it was only when the banks advised the government to use the projects for the extremely poor that the number of minorities living in the projects probably quadrupled. So, they gave us the projects when the government couldn't afford to pay up anymore. We got the leftovers. The government basically forced us to live this way. The rich got richer and the poor got poorer, and too bad the poor happened to be Blacks and a few other minorities sprinkled in here and there. And let me say that it wasn't all the Whites, but it was enough to bring about change, hurtful change that would last decades, and that will continue to exist unless those people begin to realize their power, and use it to help and not to hurt."

"Mama, it's okay. At this point, we can only use the past as a way to make progress not as a hurdle to continue to hold us back."

"What was your teacher thinking when she gave you this assignment?"

"Well actually the assignment wasn't planned. After this White kid named James said that I was poor and lazy because I was from the ghetto, Ms. Dream immediately stepped in. Instead of running away from the issue she chose to use this situation as a teachable moment."

"Yeah, well you are right about that Sydnee. A lot of teachers probably would have just moved on without discussing the issue."

"I mean that is what she is there for, to teach. I thought it was a stupid idea at first, but now that I realize how much I've learned in a day's time, I'm grateful that the whole incident happened. I mean, I had the chance to learn so much from my classmates, from all the research, and from you. I never knew my great-grandparents were a part of the very history that I am now studying. Besides, I had the chance to tell my classmates about where I am from and about how the ghetto really is. Now, they know that all Blacks aren't lazy and poor, at least I hope so. Maybe tomorrow, I will be able to teach them more important things that will help them understand us, not judge us."

"I guess baby. Just do what you know is best. You're a smart girl. I know you will hold it down."

Chapter 10:
Our Saving Grace

My mama was so angry. She could have played the role of Florida Evans better than Esther Rolle did in *Goodtimes*. And when I think about it, they did have a lot in common. They were both Black women and mothers trying to get their kids out the ghetto. I could feel the heat from my mother's blood boiling. And plus, anytime she's angry, she forgets to tell me things. She had forgotten to give me my nightly chain of commands—to take my bath, brush my teeth, say my prayers, and go to sleep. So I went ahead without her. Besides, this routine had been drilled in me.

As I relaxed in the bed, looking up at the molded swirls in the ceiling, I couldn't stop thinking about everything my mom had shared with me. Then, I heard my Granny come in from her Monday night Bingo tournament. This was her Monday night routine. Her and all the rest of the elders gathered in Ms. Flora's cramped living room and played Bingo.

"Hey, baby. Where's Sydnee?"

"She's in bed already."

"What's wrong? Did something happen at work?"

"No, mam. It's Sydnee."

"What's wrong with granny's baby?"

"I'm so upset with myself. It's all my fault. I wanted her to be the best and to have the best. Now, I done transferred her to this ritzy school, and on her first day, for the first time ever, she was teased."

"What? Why baby?"

"Well, according to Sydnee she's the only Black girl in her gifted class, and she's the only one from Magnolia Park, the ghetto…the projects?"

"Well baby, there is nothing Sydnee can do about that. She's there now. Sydnee's a smart girl. She's going to take care of the both of us one day. She's going to beat all these, here, negative odds that are working against, not only her, but all the rest of the kids from the Magnolia Parks all across this, here, country. So don't you worry about her. You did the right thing. Instead of the opportunity coming to her, you brought her to the opportunity. You did your part as a mother, and for that you will be later rejoicing and giving Him the glory. Sydnee's a strong girl. She ain't gone let them kids steal her glory, because she is going all the way, okay Karen."

"Okay, mama. I knew you'd come home and cheer me up."

"You knew I was. Now, I don't even know why you was in here sobbing and what not. Girl, clean up your face! Go on, now." I heard mama walking to the bathroom to do exactly what granny had told her to do. Then I heard granny following her. As I peeked over the covers, I could see the shadow from grandma's foot at the bathroom door. Karen, did you tell Sydnee what I used to always tell you."

"What's that, mama?"

"That God didn't make the ghetto, the government did?"

"No, I was too emotional, but I'm sure she just heard you. You know she listens to everything we say, when she's pretending to be asleep." I wanted to "Amen" that, but I didn't want them to now I was listening. I decided to let them have their moment.

Chapter 11:
You Go Girl

The bus ride to school went too slow for me. This time I didn't care about admiring the scenery. I just wanted to get to school, and fast. I was ready to see what everyone was going to share. I wanted to learn, and now!

When I got off the bus, I read over the motivational quotes on the sidewalk hoping that they would inspire me to have a good day, then I raced into the building and right into my class. Everyone was there waiting, eagerly. I could see it on their faces. I tapped on my desk, counting down as the tardy bell got ready to ring because I knew Ms. Dream would be entering soon after.

"Good morning class! Don't we all look prepared and ready to share what we've learned. I hope everyone completed their journals, as well, because I will be checking them. And besides, I am ready to begin the continuation of yesterday's lesson. I am enthusiastic as well, and I have some interesting details to share from my research, too. So, you all weren't the only ones who had homework."

I liked Ms. Dream. She wasn't your typical teacher. She did more than giving commands. She was a participant as well. She allowed us to be the teacher sometimes, too. The research that the school had given my mom when she came to register me said that this was supposed to be one of the benefits of being in a gifted class. Teachers were allowed to deviate a little from the required curriculum and teach attention-grabbing activities like this one that was sparked yesterday. Hooray, to teacher autonomy!

"Okay, who wants to go first?" I was the first person to raise my hand. "Me, Ms. Dream!"

"Okay, go on up to the podium Sydnee. I'm going to take the role while you are preparing. James, Taylor, Reagan…"

"Okay." I gathered all of my notes from my desk, and reshuffled them neatly tapping them on my desk. Then, I headed up to the wooden podium. "Good luck, Sydnee!"

"Thanks, James." I hoped Ms. Dream didn't think this podium was going to intimidate me. I've longed for the day to stand behind one these. Actually, I daydream about it all the time, especially when I think about delivering my achievement speech for finding the cure for AIDS. So, I was ready.

"Ready, Miss Sydnee?"

"Yes, I am." I had to clear my throat. It was only right. I mean you've seen the presidential addresses to the country, clearing the throat was routine. If it was good enough for them to do it, then hey, I was going to do it too. "Good morning, class and Ms. Dream."

"Good morning, Miss Sydnee."

"Well, with the help of the library and some outside help from my mom, I would have to say that I was able to base my findings that I am going to share with you all, from extensive research and very worthy references. Well, as you all discovered yesterday, I live in Magnolia Park Projects. So, of course, I researched the history of the Public Housing Authority because the term 'projects' was a derogatory term that came along much later. Well, not really so derogatory, but its connotation, or the way it sounds, just sounds bad. Yeah, I found that word in the dictionary yesterday." The class laughed at my somewhat funny joke. "The first thing I found was that the projects were originally built to house the large number of workers who worked in the city but lived in the country areas. But then, some banks got involved. The banks figured that since so many of these people were making a living, that they would help these people relocate to better areas away from the city because the city was becoming overpopulated and filthy. Just imagine the period of the Industrial Revolution. We've read about how all these jobs came about, and how workers were pouring into the city, and as we all know, the more people, the more problems. So the city began to become home to violence. So these workers, with the help of the banks, began to move out the city, into what one of you all will present…the suburbs. But that's another story. So anyways, there was no one really left to live in the public housing authority, or the projects. So then the banks came up with an idea. They advised the government to give the public housing authority, or projects, to the poor people. Since most of the Whites were already off living in the suburbs and since many of the city's workers were probably indentured servants, the extremely poor would be the Blacks and other minorities. So the Blacks and other minorities got all happy because they finally had somewhere to call home, never smelling that there was a scam. So, all the Blacks began to move into the projects. And actually my research stated that the number of Blacks and minorities living in the projects began to grow a lot. So anyhow, the projects was the place to be when everyone first began to move in. I mean they had swimming pools, hot water, heat, and elevators. To them they were living like the rich and famous. But they really weren't. They were too blind to see that while Whites were out building up equity from their little houses, they were losing money by paying the low amount of rent. Personally, I think the government set them up. I mean if you don't know, we love the hook up, and that's what they thought they were getting—low rent, free hot water and utilities, and a pool and playground for the kids. But that was a lie, especially once the government began to forget about them. So happen, the government goes broke. I mean come on. Everyone knows the government doesn't go broke. So the government says, 'We can't afford to pay for the repairs that you all need.' Then they go on to say that, 'They should have been grateful and taken care of their community. Didn't we do them a favor? We give them free water, the least they can do is pay for their own repairs?' So, what was once good becomes bad. All of the projects begin to overload in the amount of repairs they need. Windows are broken. Doors are broken. Elevators no longer work, and the water no longer gets hot because, now, the furnace is broken too. So as you can see the projects went through, what I call, metamorphosis. And to make it worse, they began to build highways in the city, which added to the negative feel for the city. The interstates were viewed as the escape routes away from the city. And all those overpasses, which run through my neighborhood, those were built for people to "look down" on us as they passed over and still pass over in their fancy cars. Like my granny always says, 'Look up to heaven and down for hel'…well do you all catch my drift."

"Yeah, interesting," James said.

"And that's what we were, at least us who lived in the projects…the slum, the city, the poor, the Black. The End."

When I got done everyone sat in awe. You would have thought Dr. King, himself, had come back from heaven and delivered that speech by the way their faces were looking. Even Ms. Dream looked mesmerized. Then I heard someone began to clap. I looked up and it was Taylor, then Reagan, then James, and before long, it was the entire class.

"That was great Sydnee. But remember, we can't attempt to use the h-word in school, okay. Very informative, that was good. I liked the way you brought your emotions into it, and spoke from the heart. That was great. Okay let's move on, we are going to save our questions until the end. Does anyone want to volunteer to go next?"

Chapter 12:
Back Live from the Suburbs

No one raised their hand. You'd think that there would be more leaders considering that this was a gifted class, but I guess all smart people aren't leaders. As I finished my thought, I could hear James shuffling in his seat behind me. I knew he wanted to go next. When I turned to look at him, it was written all over his face. "I will!" I knew it. James probably had a lot to share with us. I was good.

"Okay, class let's give James our undivided attention." I just wondered, what, did he find out. I wonder is he going to talk about any of the things my mama had told me?

"Okay, before I begin I would like to say that I no longer feel like this little rich White kid from River Rouge. From all of my researching, and after talking it over with my mom, I can honestly say that I feel privileged. And I think that I will look at African Americans and other minorities in a totally different light now. But, I will say that I am not blaming myself or all of my ancestors for what has happened because this is larger than the act of some persons, these are the acts of many powerful people." Maybe his mom had told him some of the same things that my mom had told me, I thought.

"When I first began to research the suburbs, I actually thought I was going to find some very positive research about how this place is home to happy American families. Well I did, but that wasn't all I found.

When I shared this information with my parents I thought they would be stunned. Well my dad was, but my mom wasn't. She had already known about everything I was sharing with them. To my surprise, her great-grandmother was an abolitionist, and an abolitionist was a White person who was against slavery. Instead of persecuting the slaves back in the day, she secretly would teach them to read and write. My mom said she was totally against slavery. But coming back to the subject matter, my dad thought it was all a lie. He detested it all, but my mother quickly made him come to his senses. As she said, she refreshed his memory." We all laughed.

"Well, when I first began my search, all these websites for first time home owners popped up, but I knew this wasn't going to tell me anything. So then I searched, the history of suburbs, and all of a sudden it hit me, I had hit the jackpot. Tons of information came up with a lot of different subheadings—White flight, blockbusting, redlining, racial segregation. I was shocked. I didn't know what to click on, so I decided to click on the one about the first American suburb called Bevittstown. I thought this one would be interesting.

Like I previously stated, Bevittstown was the first American suburb, and it has been recognized as the ideal American suburb. It was the ideal of a bright and talented man named William Bevitt, and I will talk about him a little later on. So anyhow, in Bevittstown's earlier days, it was home to more than eighty thousand Americans, most of who were soldiers who had just come home from World War II. But out of all these eighty thousand people, I must note that not one of them was African American or Japanese American or Latino American. Bevittstown was inhabited by one group of people and those were the Caucasians. With the help of banks, these homes were made very affordable, especially for the soldiers and their families. Bevittstown was located about fifty miles outside of New York City. Mr. Bevitt thought that this little suburb would be best here because the city was turning into a slum and becoming very overcrowded, especially with the job boom. Bevittstown attracted newly married young families. It was supposed to be the hot thing, the American Dream with the white house and the picket fence. Because there were so many people living here, Mr. Bevitt didn't want his town to look anything like the city. So he decided to make neighborhoods within Levittstown. You know like the ones around here. We have River Rouge, River Park, The Plantations, and so on." Oh, yeah I thought. I recall seeing those on my ride to school yesterday. "But Mr. Bevitt called these little neighborhoods village centers, hoping that this would hold his idea of the community together. Each of the village centers came with swimming pools, play grounds, basketball courts, and community centers. As you can see, Mr. Bevitt's purpose was to stress the importance of community and family, unlike it was stressed in the city. In the city there wasn't much of a sense of community. There wasn't much for families to go out and enjoy because there was nothing but old factories, and who would want to go see some old polluted factories? And let me add that these houses were easy to build because there were only like three different styles, so building them was no problem. To those workers, it probably came to them like writing our name comes for us. The End."

"Good James. We're running out of time class. Anyone else? Any questions?"

Chapter 13:
Answers to Her Questions

Chastity raised her head up from her desk and pulled her arm from out her blue wool sweater. Oh, my God. This was the first time I ever saw her raise her hand, but it was only the second day of school. Chastity seemed to be very quiet. She looked mix, with what, I didn't know. She had long curly Black hair, with fairly light skin. It looked like she had a tan. She was very neatly dressed, and for the first time she was talking.

"Well, why weren't the African Americans or anyone else from other races allowed to live in Bevittstown? I mean, that's not fair. They fought in the war too."

"James, do you want to answer that?"

"Sure. Well, Chastity, according to my research there were a lot of things that took place that were not fair, not only for Blacks, but for other races, as well. There really wasn't much they could do especially when there were different forms of discrimination going on."

Chastity raised her hand. "Just how many forms of discrimination are there. I never heard of that before."

"Good question, Chastity."

Ms. Dream walked from where she was standing, "Class, these are the kinds of questions I want you to ask. They open the dialogue for learning. Great job! I love it!"

"Well, from my research there is individual discrimination or racism that a single person may display. There's group discrimination that can be displayed amongst people of the same interest. Then, there is institutional discrimination, which is harder to change. It happens when a more powerful or majority group discriminates against a group that is not as powerful. With this type of discrimination, the discrimination comes off more subtly and less obvious."

"Can you give us an example James?" Asked Ms. Dream.

"Okay...some historical ones could be Jim Crow laws because which required separate for Whites and Blacks. The group of power would unfortunately be the government and the less powerful would be Blacks. Or, do you remember the Black guy who was brutally beat by the police in Detroit? The tapes showed that the cops were guilty. But the charges were dropped because somehow the trial was moved to Southfield, which was an area with less Blacks, which meant less Blacks would probably be in the jury. The power group was the court system the less powerful group the citizens. We'd be here all day if I kept going."

I was in awe, I never knew discrimination was so big.

"Good job, James. And to piggyback on what James was stating, institutional discrimination is probably the most powerful form of discrimination there is. And let me add, institutional discrimination shows prejudice by one's sex, gender, language, religion, culture, class, or status. Do you all get what I'm saying by institutional discrimination?"

"Yes, I guess," said Reagan.

"Okay, can someone give me an example of a form of institutional discrimination?"

"Okay, I have another one, said James. My mom said that even today, some banks have been found guilty of charging minorities higher interest rates on home loans than they do for Whites."

"That's a good one, James. Does anyone else know of any?" said Ms. Dream.

"Well, Ms. Dream I was reading an article in the newspaper the other day, and it was talking about how some tests that we will have to take to get into college are unfair to Blacks and minorities."

"Okay, Sydnee explain to me and the class how some test makers can end up serving as agents of institutional discrimination."

"Well, if Blacks and other minorities perform low on these tests then we will not be able to be accepted to the best schools like Harvard, Yale, Vanderbilt, or MIT."

"Okay, keep going."

"Ummm…, as we all know these are the best universities and colleges, so if we aren't able to go to the 'best' schools, which means we will not be able to get the 'best' education. My mom says that people who go to Ivy League and other big name school oftentimes get the better jobs and get paid more than those who may pursue the same major at less affluent schools."

"You're right, Sydnee. That has been none to occur. I can relate to that. I attended an HBCU, which stands for Historically Black Colleges and Universities in Nashville, Tennessee, and my best friend attended Teachers College in New York. I wanted to go there too, but my test scores were much lower than hers. When I graduated, I had a perfect grade point average, and she had a 'B' grade point average. We both applied for a job at this prep school on the East Coast. She got the job, and I didn't."

"I don't mean to be rude, but I'm glad you didn't get the job or you wouldn't be here with us, Ms. Dream."

"You're right Sydnee. But class, I don't want you all to be ignorant to what really happens sometimes. It may not be fair, but it does happen. Maybe it doesn't happen all the time, but once is enough."

Surprisingly, Chastity raised her hand again. "I know one, Ms. Dream."

"Okay let's hear it, Chastity."

"On the news last night, the news anchor was talking about how some of the people in the lower working classes don't get health benefits even though they work full-time jobs. And she went on to add that most of these people were minorities. So to make a long story short, the insurance companies and the employers, or the companies that the workers work for, would be the agents of institutional discrimination."

"Why so, Chastity?"

"Because if the minority workers aren't able to get the insurance benefits, they will not be able to get the proper healthcare that they need to fight off diseases. So that's would be institutional discrimination from the healthcare too, a little. Right?"

"That's good Chastity. I am so glad that we had the chance to talk about these issues because you know, a lot of teachers wouldn't dare teach about this. But who cares about them, that's what I'm here for, to be a dare devil. But before you all go home and tell your parents that, 'Ms. Dream said this about institutional discrimination…' Not all cases of institutional discrimination are intentional, or done on purpose. That's the key, and that's why it is so powerful. Institutions can also use subtle forms of discrimination, and with subtle forms of discrimination, the intent is not intentional. But because so many people are affected by it, it becomes obvious and strong. And to me that explains the difference degree of racism and discrimination. Racism is intentional, but discrimination can be either intentional or unintentional."

"So institutional discrimination is not always done by bad people," asked James.

"Or racist people?" I asked.

"You both are right, Mr. James and Miss Sydnee. I see you all are working better and better together by the day."

"Yep."

"Oh, yeah Ms. Dream, I wrote a poem. Is it okay if I read it?"

"Okay you can read it, but afterwards class I will give you some other important terms that go along with the issues we are discussing. We don't have time to go over each one, but I want you all to have them for just FYI, for your information."

Chapter 14:
For Your Information

"Okay, that's a deal!" exclaimed James.

"Quickly class, get out a pen and paper?"

Again we said in unison, "A PEN?"

"Yes, you all are gifted, and in this class we write with pens."

Then, here goes James. "Oh yeah, we forgot about that Ms. Dream, we are dare-devils."

"Exactly. Okay the first word is, white flight, w-h-i-t-e, f-l-i-g-h-t, white flight. And white flight describes the migration of Whites from suburban areas because there was a fear that minorities were moving in which would make them lose money on their house. At the same time Blacks and other minorities migrated from the city to the suburbs in hopes of acquiring bigger houses, higher property value, more equity, and a more peaceful life. But some research shows that although they may get the bigger houses, they don't always get more equity. In most cases, many minorities were being charged higher interest rates than their White counterparts. So ultimately they paid more for the same homes that Whites paid less for. This definition leads us into the next definition, redlining.

"R-e-d-l-i-n-i-n-g, redlining. Redlining has caused serious problems for African-American and other low-income communities. In the past, banks would draw maps of particular areas. Then they would draw red lines around areas that they just decided they didn't want to lend or give money to anymore. As a result, people who moved into these areas would pay more for services like banking, getting loans, or insurance. Just say you get a loan for one thousand dollars. Now, you have no clue that you live in an area that has been redlined, or that you are being charged a higher interest rate. By the time you end up paying the loan off, you probably have paid more than two thousand dollars back. Now, that's unfair, and that is redlining."

"That is unfair," said James.

"Well James, these practices by some banks are very deceptive, and nothing more than scams. Redlining turns one's dream of home ownership into a nightmare, and in the worst instances, these people home ownership dreams have ended in foreclosure, meaning they lose their houses, which ultimately makes unstable neighborhoods even more unstable.

Does everyone else understand?" We all shook our heads in agreement.

"Number three, is blockbusting. I'm not going to spell this one for you. Spell block, and then bust, and add —i-n-g. Blockbusting is the illegal practice of advising homeowners to sell their property by making remarks or indications regarding the entry of persons of a particular race or national origin into the neighborhood. On a lighter note, because I know that probably just went, right, over your heads. Let me give you all an example. James just bought himself a new house in Beverly Hills. He lives there for about two years. He and his family love this house. They never want to move. Besides their equity is steadily growing, more money. So, Sydnee and her husband decide that they want to move in Beverly Hills. And Tu decides to move there as well. So, that is how many minority families moving to Beverly Hills, class?"

"Two," we all said.

"Okay, I just wanted to make sure you all were paying attention. So anyways, that's only two families. So, James' realtor calls him up one day. 'Hi, James, how's it going?'

'Great, Bob. We love it here!'

'Well, I have some bad news for you. Two minority families, just closed on some houses in your neighborhood, one African American and another family from Japan. I hate to break it to you, but I think you'd better pack up your family and get ready to move.'

'Why, Bob. I'd love to have some new neighbors. Do they have kids? Okay, good. That will be great for the twins!'

'James, I'm afraid you don't understand. If you don't move you are going to lose money on your house. You will lose thousands. I'm sure you don't want to do that. Besides, if you move the bank will help you out. You will be able to move in that new exclusive country club subdivision east of Beverly Hills that they're building. As a matter of fact, they're almost done. Plus, a house in that neighborhood would be worth twice as much as yours. It's your choice. But if it was me, I'd take the ticket out and move, before more of them move in.'

"Now, class, if James moves he would be participating in blockbusting because he was tipped off to move before Sydnee and Tu moved in with their families. And James' realtor, Bob, was carrying out blockbusting all the way."

"Well, that's crazy. I wouldn't dare move," said James. "I'd keep my family and me right there!"

"But, even not for the money, James? You would be getting twice as much?"

"I know Maxwell, but in this case it's about morals. If I moved, I would only be adding to the problem. If more families, remained steadfast in the homes they already had, then none of this would be going on to date."

"Yeah, Maxwell," I said. "It's not always about the money. It's about morals."

"No, Sydnee, it's about the values, if you know what I mean." I could have slapped him. He was being so insensitive.

"Okay, class. Let's get back on task. Many people would have a hard time deciding on rather to choose money or morals."

"Ms. Dream, my grandmother told me that that was how Eight Mile Road came about." Everyone's head turned toward James waiting for him to say another word, to explain how?

"How, James?" said Ms. Dream.

"From what you just described to us,…from blockbusting. Her best friend, Ms. Mary, used to live in a neighborhood just south of Eight Mile. And she said that around the early 40s a lot of Blacks began to move into the city north of Eight Mile, and at the same time many Whites began to move away. So, she said eventually realtors came to them and told them that if they didn't move or do something fast, then the value of their homes were going to lose their value. So, she said that one of her neighbors built a brick wall separating the neighborhood south of Eight Mile or the White side, from the neighborhoods north of Eight Mile known as the Black side."

"Is that so, James? Will someone go and do a search on the history of Eight Mile for me?"

"I will Ms. Dream!"

I ran over to the computer. I wanted to know if this was really true. This just could not be happening in my own city, not Detroit. As I typed in the Eight Mile Road, tons of links popped up. Some about state lines. Some on Motown. "Bingo! I found something, Ms. Dream."

"Read it for us, Sydnee."

"Well initially, Eight Mile came from the Land Ordinance Act of 1785. And in this act, a line was drawn from Michigan's east to west lakeshores, and this line became known as the Eight Mile Road that we know today. It is a county line that goes across the state, and after jumping over Lake Michigan, Eight Mile becomes the state line separating Illinois and Wisconsin."

"Does it say anything about the subject matter that we're discussing?"

I hit the back arrow, and scanned back over the Eight Mile links. "Okay, I found one."

"Summarize it for us because we don't have much time, we have to get ready for science, and James has to recite his poem."

"According to this brief document called Creative Partners to reclaim Detroit, Eight Mile is considered the urban, suburban divide in Detroit, and it is among the most severe cases of racial segregation in the nation. Not only are there tensions between the residents of the city and the suburbs, but there are also tensions between the politicians, as well. You would think that by them being the political leaders that they would try to set the examples for their citizens. But I guess not. Ummm…it also says that residents in the suburbs are afraid to cross Eight Mile's boundaries. To them, crossing Eight Mile is taking a huge risk. Oh, I can't summarize this. It's taking too long. Can I just read it, Ms. Dream."

"Okay."

"It states that, "To many suburban dwellers, Detroit has become home to the poor, drug addicts, predators, the old, the sick, the single parent, and the at-risk. The city's population has decreased since the 1950s and white flight has been a common thing since the 1967 riots. Eight out of nine Blacks live in Detroit's inner city, while eight out of nine Whites live in the suburbs.""

"Good, Sydnee. I loved the way you read so clearly."

"So, that's bad huh, Ms. Dream?"

"Well, yeah, James in a way."

"We have to do something we just can't let this continue to happen. Now that we know about all these issues, we must inform the people. Everyone can't know this is going on."

"No, I'm sure they don't, James, at least not everyone. Well class, I have enjoyed this lesson, and I'm sure you all have as well. We have all learned a lot about this country's history, the suburbs, the ghetto, and about our own city of Detroit. But now, we have only a couple of minutes left before, the bell rings for lunch. When we get back, we are going to start science, and I'm serious. No more of this topic. We have to move on. Besides you all can't be gifted and well-rounded if we only stick to one subject, can you?" We all laughed. "James, are you ready to read your poem?"

"Ready, Ms. Dream."

"Class, are you ready?" Again in unison we said, "Yes, Ms. Dream!"

"Okay, hit it James."

"Okay, I wrote this poem just for this occasion. I hope it makes us all think, and I hope it makes us all forgiving of each others' ignorance, shortcomings, and things that we just cannot change about each other our race, religion, gender, language, class, and culture. Okay here it goes…

I don't know what caused my decision
It shouldn't matter what color, race or religion…that
someone is
It's okay for you to hold a huge grudge
Deep inside I know there was no reason to actually judge
Just because of your upbringing and environment
Now I see none of that matters because you are so content
With who you are, what you are and where you will go
I now understand that I shouldn't comment on anything
unless I know
The complete story behind the person and not just off an
assumption
Oh Yeah! Thanks in advance for the help with the Trig function
Getting to know you has been good & you helped me
realize
A lot about myself, so to you Sydnee…I apologize!"

Chapter 15:
A Happy Ending

That was some school. Tameka and Michele are right, Cadillac Magnet was an awesome school. Maybe I'll go back and visit one day. I can't believe that when it was all over, James and I with the help of Ms. Dream, helped revitalize the city of Detroit. Through our service-learning project, *Making Detroit ONE*, we went out and educated the people of the city and the suburbs about the very things that we had learned in our 7th grade classroom. Because of us, the people in Detroit, the White and the Black, came together as one community, one neighborhood. A few months after our service-learning project, the city council and school board were very proud of our work and effort to change Detroit. So they gave James and I, as well as Ms. Dream, a service-learning award. Eight Mile was given an alias, *Sydnee James Boulevard* in honor of James and I, two very powerful students who both had big voices and big dreams. Our big dreams followed us throughout our public school journey. James and I, both attended the same high school. He was salutatorian, and I was valedictorian. At our graduation, we were in for the surprise of our life. Ms. Dream, our seventh grade teacher who was responsible for our great service-learning project, was there to honor us. She read all of the honors and awards that both of us had received. The entire school was proud of us, as well as our parents and Ms. Dream. I still keep in touch with James.

After leaving Cadillac Magnet, we became the best of friends, and our friendship still lives on. We see each other all the time at frat parties. Yeah, I said frat parties. We are only a few miles from each other. He's an electrical engineering major at MIT, and I'm a pre-med major at Harvard. We are both living our dreams…the American Dream.

Printed in the United States
72426LV00005B/481-528